my zoo

Rod Campbell

Collins
An Imprint of HarperCollins*Publishers*

The elephant is big and strong.

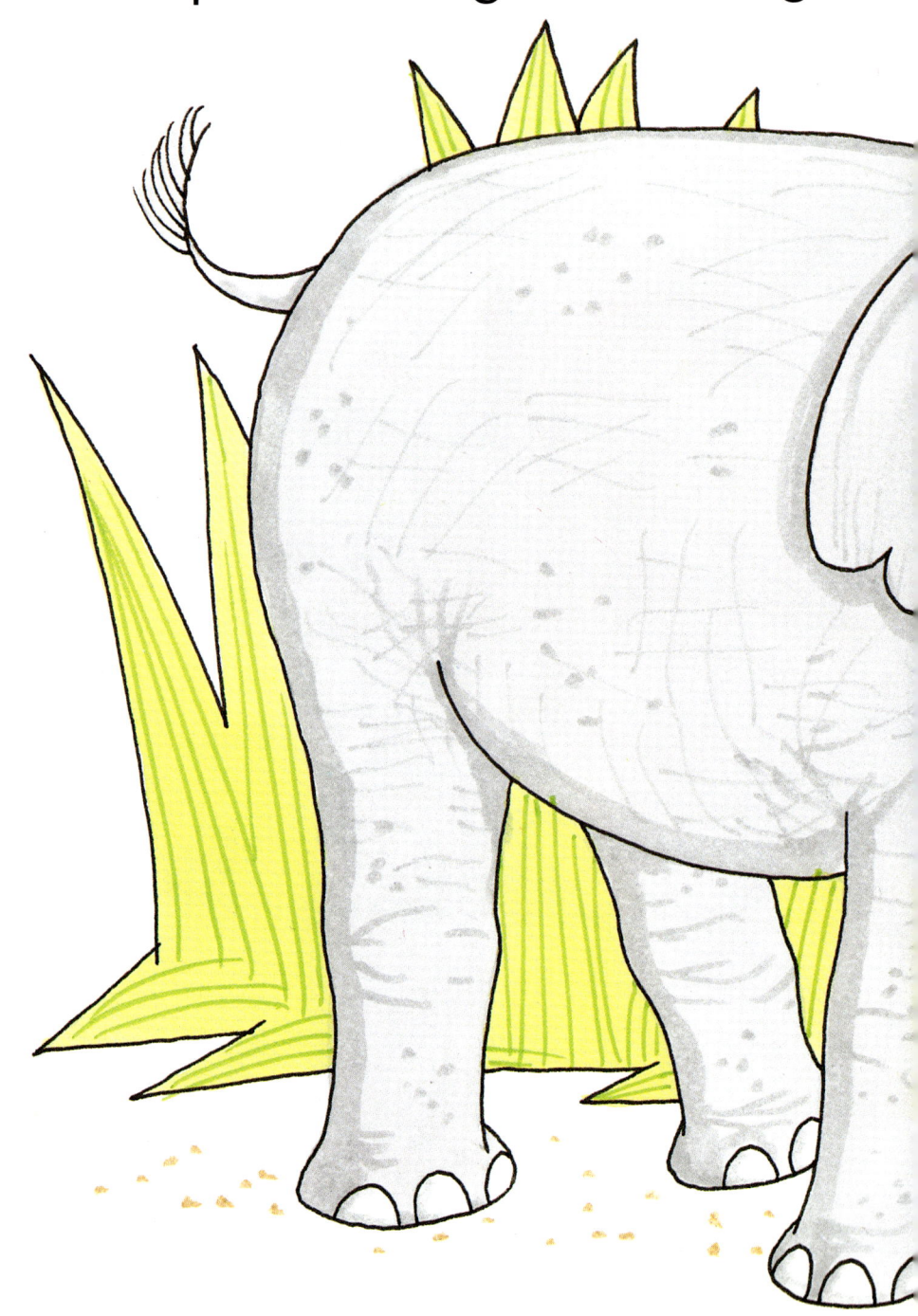

The lion is sleeping after his dinner.

lamp

ice-cream

orange

net

The snake is long and thin.

The giraffe has a very long neck.

5

4

3

2

1

The monkeys swing in the trees.

The parrots are very noisy.

The crocodile has very sharp teeth.

The kangaroo carries its baby in a pouch.

The polar bear likes swimming.

The tiger is hot and thirsty.

elephant
lion
snake
giraffe
monkey
parrot
crocodile
kangaroo
polar bear
tiger

First published in Great Britain
by Collins Children's Division,
part of HarperCollins Publishers Limited.

3 5 7 9 10 8 6 4 2

isbn 0 00 100647 9 (book & tape pack)